This Little Tiger book belongs to:

_____

_____

_____

_____

700029445802

For Helen, with love
~ P B

For Tom and Emily
~ M B

LITTLE TIGER PRESS
An imprint of Magi Publications
1 The Coda Centre, 189 Munster Road, London SW6 6AW
www.littletigerpress.com

First published in Great Britain 2005
This edition published 2006

A CIP catalogue record for this book
is available from the British Library

All rights reserved • ISBN 1 84506 106 3

Printed in Belgium by Proost N.V.

10 9 8 7 6 5 4 3 2 1

Nobody Laughs at a Lion!

Paul Bright   Illustrated by Matt Buckingham

Little Tiger Press

London

In the cool of the morning,
on the edge of the jungle, the
animals were busy as can be.
They were running and racing,
climbing and clambering, crawling
and creeping all over the place.
Pa Lion sat and watched.

"You can see why I'm King of the Jungle," he said. "It's because I'm the best."

"Do stop boasting," said Ma Lion. "And if you are the best, what are you best at?"

Pa Lion thought for a while.

"Well, running for a start. You just watch."
Pa Lion bounded off through the long grass,
sending the other animals scattering in fright.

As Pa Lion ran, the sleek, long-legged
Cheetah raced past him with ease, and
Cheetah laughed. He laughed quietly,
because nobody laughs out loud at a lion.
But Pa Lion heard him.

"All right," said Pa Lion, rather annoyed.
"Cheetah might be just a little bit
better at running. But I'm best at . . .
at climbing trees. Look!"

Pa Lion dug his great claws into the nearest tree and scrambled and scratched and scrabbled, and slowly heaved himself up on to the lowest branch.

"Of course, some trees are more difficult to climb than others," he said.

Monkey was swinging by his tail in the highest branches of the tree, and he saw Pa Lion climbing and he sniggered. He sniggered quietly, because nobody sniggers out loud at a lion. But Pa Lion heard him.

"All right," said Pa Lion, grumpily.
"Monkey might be just a little bit better
at climbing trees. But I'm the best at . . .
at creeping through the long grass, quiet as quiet."

Pa Lion dropped into a low crouch, then, crawling and creeping, slow as slow and quiet as quiet, he moved through the long grass.

Snake was slipping through the grass, smooth and silent as a sigh. He saw Pa Lion crawling and creeping, and he smiled.

He smiled to himself, because nobody
smiles at a lion. But Pa Lion saw him.

Pa Lion was beginning to feel angry. "All right," he said. "Snake might be just a little bit better at creeping through the long grass, quiet as quiet. But I am the best at . . . at . . ."

"You are very good at sleeping," said Ma Lion.

"Sleeping doesn't count," said Pa Lion.

Then he said, "I am the strongest. Watch me."
He pushed his great head against the trunk of a small tree, bending it until it broke with a loud crack!

Elephant was plodding past, leaving
a trail of flattened bushes and broken
trees in his path.

He saw Pa Lion and he lifted his trunk
and trumpeted. He trumpeted softly,
because not even an elephant trumpets
out loud at a lion. But Pa Lion heard him.

Now Pa Lion was furious. "All right," he said. "Maybe
Elephant is just a little bit stronger. But I am the best
at . . . the best at . . . Oh! I can't think of anything!

"It really makes me want to . . .

"... ROAR!"

And the sound of Pa Lion's roar rolled and rumbled and grew and grumbled and echoed and thundered through the jungle.

Pa Lion really *was* the very, very best at roaring.

Cheetah stopped laughing, and Monkey stopped sniggering, and Snake stopped smiling, and Elephant stopped trumpeting.

And Pa Lion was happy at last . . . because
NOBODY laughs at a lion!

Roaring good reads from Little Tiger Press

While Angels Watch

Marni McGee Tina Macnaughton

AUGUSTUS AND HIS SMILE

CATHERINE RAYNER

The BIGGEST BADDEST WOLF

Nick Ward

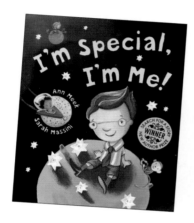

I'm Special, I'm Me!

Ann Meek
Sarah Massini

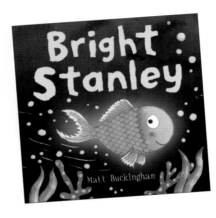

Bright Stanley

Matt Buckingham

ELIZABETH BAGULEY

MEGGIE MOON

Illustrated by GREGOIRE MABIRE

For information regarding any of the above titles
or for our catalogue, please contact us:
Little Tiger Press, 1 The Coda Centre,
189 Munster Road, London SW6 6AW, UK
Tel: 020 7385 6333 Fax: 020 7385 7333
E-mail: info@littletiger.co.uk www.littletigerpress.com